Hello Kitty®

Hello Love!

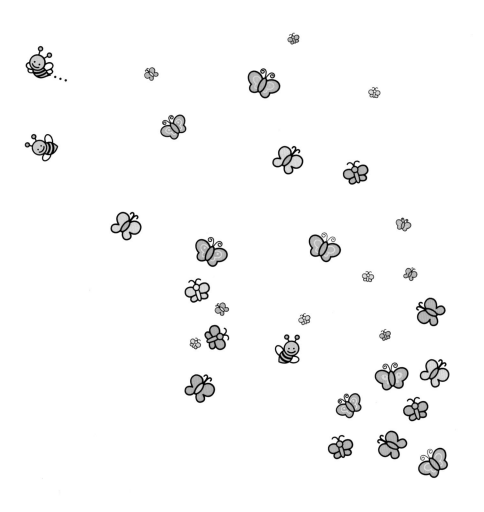

Hello Kitty

Hello Love!

illustrated and designed by
Roger La Borde and Rob Biddulph

ABRAMS BOOKS FOR YOUNG READERS
NEW YORK

Hello Kitty loves to give presents to her friends.
Today she is planning to give a present to Dear
Daniel, her very special friend.

What will Dear Daniel love as a present? Hello Kitty telephones each of her other friends for ideas!

Hello Kitty loves rainbows, and her friend
Joey loves rainbows too!

But how will Hello Kitty ever be able to wrap a rainbow?

Hello Kitty loves butterflies,
and her friend Fifi loves
butterflies too!

But butterflies love to
flutter and fly free, not be
wrapped as presents!

Hello Kitty loves warm breezes, and her friend Tippy loves warm breezes too!

But how will Hello Kitty squeeze a breeze into a box?

Hello Kitty loves to hear birds singing, and her friends Timmy and Tammy love to hear birds singing too!

But the birds sing in trees, not when they are trapped inside boxes!

Hello Kitty loves the feeling of squishy mud between her toes, and her friend Mory loves the feeling of squishy mud between his toes too.

But Dear Daniel would not love all that mud in his house, and besides, who would want a box full of mud?

**Hello Kitty wants to make Dear Daniel happy.
What will she do?**

There are so many, many things she and her
friends love, but what will Dear Daniel love?

Suddenly Hello Kitty has an idea *she* loves!

And she hopes Dear Daniel will love it too!

Hello Kitty is making a present that is like a rainbow.
It is full of singing birds and fluttering butterflies.

It is a place where warm breezes blow and where there is always plenty of mud for squishing between toes. Can you guess what it is?

Her present to Dear Daniel is a garden!
Dear Daniel loves his present from
Hello Kitty!

Illustration and Design: Roger La Borde and Rob Biddulph

The Library of Congress has cataloged the original edition of this book as follows:

La Borde, Roger.
Hello Kitty, hello love! / by Roger La Borde.
p. cm.
Summary: Hello Kitty tries to think of just the right gift for her special friend,
one that includes all the things she and her friends like.
ISBN 0-8109-8538-1
[1. Gifts—Fiction. 2. Friendship—Fiction. 3. Cats—Fiction.] I. Title.
PZ7.L1155 He 2003
[E]—dc21
2002014070

ISBN of this edition: 978-1-4197-1249-4

SIL-3456

Printed and bound in China
10 9 8 7 6 5 4 3 2 1

115 West 18th Street
New York, NY 10011
www.abramsbooks.com

HELLO KITTY.

HELLO KITTY.

HELLO KITTY

HELLO KITTY

Hello _____!

Hello _____!

Hello _____!

Hello _____!